KT-449-555

AESOP'S FABLES

Illustrated by Safaya Salter

Retold by Anne Gatti

Dedication
For Amelia

Acknowledgement
My thanks go to Jillie Speed, for her help and encouragement

Pavilion Classics edition first published in 1998

This edition first published in Great Britain in 1992 by
PAVILION BOOKS LIMITED
London House, Great Eastern Wharf,
Parkgate Road, London SW11 4NQ

Designed by Bet Ayer

A CIP catalogue record for this book is available from the British Library.

ISBN 1 86205 215 8

Printed and bound in Spain by Bookprint S.L.

2 4 6 8 10 9 7 5 3 1

This book can be ordered direct from the publisher.
Please contact the Marketing Department. But try your bookshop first.

CONTENTS

A Bird in the Hand 8
The Lion and the Mouse 9
The Beetle's Revenge 10
The Boy who cried 'Wolf!' 12
The Fox and the Goat 13
The Too-Fat Fox 14
The Wolf in Sheep's Clothing 16
The Town Mouse and the Country Mouse 17
The Proud Cockerel 19
The Stag and the Lion 20
The Cautious Fox 21
Big and Little Fish 22
The Lion's Share 24
The Woodmen and the Axe 25
The Lion and the Elephant 26
How theTortoise got its Shell 28
The Hidden Treasure 28
A Lesson in Strength 29
The Noisy Frog 29
The Caged Bird 30
The Miser 32
The Hares and the Frogs 33
The Foolish Mice 34
The Frogs without a King 36
The Spendthrift and the Swallow 37
The Camel 37

The Clever Dog 38
The Proud Fir Tree 40
The Dog, the Cock and the Fox 41
The Jackdaw who Cheated 42
The Frog and the Land Rat 44
The Ambitious Jackdaw 45
The Fox and the Stork 46
Two of a Kind 48
The Monkey and the Fisherman 48
The Shepherd's Mistake 49
The Selfish Horse 49
The Grateful Eagle 50
The Crow and the Gods 52
Something out of Nothing 52
The Parrot and the Cat 53
The Dog in the Manger 54
The Lioness and the Vixen 56
An Ass in a Lion's Skin 57
The Pig and the Sheep 57
The Wise Martin 58
Mercury and the Woodman 60
The Goose that laid the Golden Eggs 61
The Mean Bees 62
The Crab and her Son 64
The Traveller and Fortune 64
The Hawk, the Kite and the Pigeons 65
The Jealous Camel 66
The Man and his Wig 68
The Cat's True Nature 68
The Exiled Jackdaw 69
The Wise Cicada 70
The Crab and the Fox 72
The Greedy Ant 73

The Fox and the Mask 74
The Boy Bathing 76
The Frogs and the Well 76
The Shipwreck 77
The Two Thieves 77
The Greedy Dog 78
A Lesson in Humility 80
The Dishonest Doctor 80
The Fox and the Grapes 81
The Wild Boar and the Fox 81
The Determined Tortoise 82
The Pack-Ass and the Wild Ass 84
The Bear's Message 85
The Ant and the Dove 86
The Ass and the Wolf 88
The Gundog and the Hare 89
The Reed and the Olive Tree 90
The Grasshopper and the Ants 92
Jumping to Conclusions 93
The Bald Man 93
When a Man Means Business 94
True Friends 96
The Belly and the Feet 96
The Sun and the Wind 97
The Foolish Crow 98
The Ass and His Burdens 100
The Frog's Words of Wisdom 101
The Flute-Playing Wolf 102
The Amaranth and the Rose 104
The Stammering Hunter 104
The Gnat's Sticky End 105

About the Author 107

A BIRD IN THE HAND

A LION found a hare asleep and was about to eat it when he spotted a deer running by. He left the hare to chase after the deer, but he made so much noise that the hare woke up and ran away.

After a long chase the lion realized that he was not going to catch up with the deer. He returned to where the hare had been, only to find that it, too, had fled.

'Serves me right,' said the lion, 'for leaving the food that I had under my nose in the hope of getting something bigger.'

MORAL

Be happy with what you've got.

THE LION AND THE MOUSE

A SLEEPING lion was woken by a mouse runnng over his face. He grabbed it with his paw and was on the point of eating it when the frightened mouse squeaked: 'Please don't kill me. If you let me go I will repay you one day.' The lion was so amused by the idea of a mouse being able to do anything for him that he just laughed and let it go. One day, however, the lion got caught in a trap prepared by a hunter. He struggled to free himself, but just got more entangled in the net. He roared with anger, and the mouse, recognizing his voice, immediately came running. Without having to be asked, the mouse set about gnawing through the ropes, and soon the lion was freed. 'You see?' said the mouse. 'You laughed at me when I promised to repay you, but you needed my help after all.'

MORAL

There are times when even the strongest may need the help of the weak.

THE BEETLE'S REVENGE

A HARE who was being chased by an eagle was completely exhausted and in dire need of help. The only creature he could see nearby was a beetle, so he begged the little insect to help him. The beetle told him not to worry, she would protect him. Just then the eagle swooped down, and the beetle called out to her to leave the poor hare alone. But the mighty eagle, scornful of such a tiny creature, tore the hare to pieces right before the beetle's eyes.

The beetle was furious and promised herself that she would pay the eagle back for ignoring her request. She watched the eagle closely to find out where she made her nests, and every time she laid some eggs, the beetle flew up and tipped them out so that they broke.

The eagle was driven mad trying to find a nesting-site that was out of the beetle's reach. Eventually she went to Zeus and begged him to give her, his own sacred bird, a safe place to hatch her chicks.

Zeus allowed her to lay her eggs in his lap. But the beetle saw her. She made a ball of dung, flew high above where Zeus was sitting and dropped it straight into his lap. Without stopping to think, Zeus got up to shake it off and tipped out all the eggs.

MORAL

Don't be fooled by size. A small person can be just as clever as a big person.

THE BOY WHO CRIED 'WOLF!'

A YOUNG shepherd grew bored while watching his flock near a village. He decided to amuse himself by pretending that a wolf was attacking his sheep, and shouted very loudly, 'Wolf! wolf!' The villagers came running to help, only to find the shepherd boy laughing at them. He did this on several occasions, and each time the villagers came to help but found no wolf. One day wolves really did come, and again the boy was heard crying for help. He had done it once too often, however, and this time the villagers just ignored him. No help came, and there was nothing he could do to prevent the wolves from carrying off his sheep.

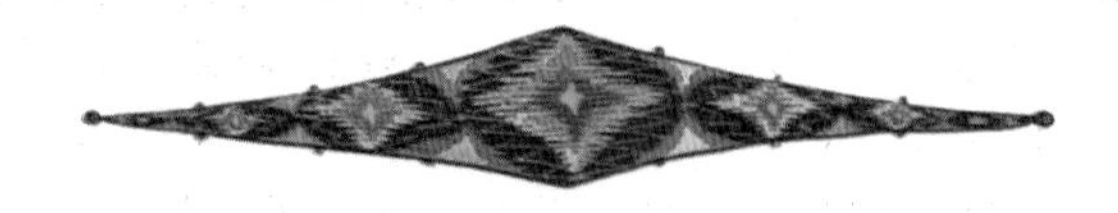

MORAL

When once you have lied, you can't expect to be believed.

THE FOX AND THE GOAT

A FOX fell into a water tank and couldn't get out. Later a thirsty goat came along and, seeing the fox in the tank, asked him whether the water was good to drink. 'It's great,' said the cunning fox. 'Why don't you come in and try it?' Without further thought the goat jumped into the tank and began to drink. Only when he had quenched his thirst did he start to look for a way to get out, but he couldn't find one. Then the fox said that he had a plan. 'I know,' he said. 'You stand on your hind legs, with your front legs pressed against the wall. I'll climb on to your back and up on to your horns. Once I'm out I'll help you get out too.' The goat did as he suggested, and the fox stepped on to his back and climbed out, but then just started to walk away. 'Hey!' shouted the goat, 'what about helping me get out, then?' The fox turned round and said, 'If you had as much sense in your head as you have hairs in your beard you wouldn't have got into the tank without thinking how you were going to get out again.'

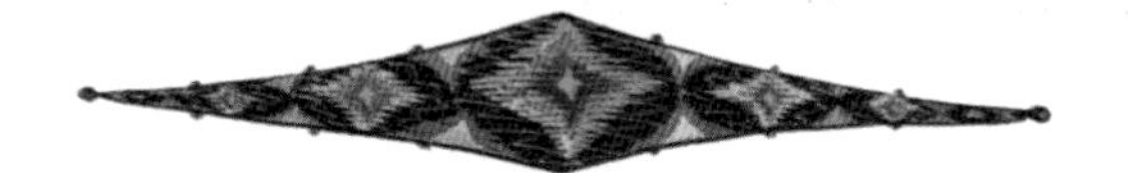

MORAL

Look before you leap.

THE TOO-FAT FOX

A HALF-STARVED fox spotted some bread and meat, which had been left in the hollow of an oak tree by shepherds. He crept inside the tree and ate every last crumb. But when he had finished he found that his stomach had swelled up so much that he could not get out.

Another fox, who was passing by, heard his cries for help and came up to ask what was the matter. 'Well,' he said, 'I suggest you stay there until you're thin again. Then you'll get out quite easily.'

MORAL

Time is a great healer.

THE WOLF IN SHEEP'S CLOTHING

A HUNGRY wolf decided to use a disguise in order to get among a flock of sheep without being noticed. He covered himself in a sheepskin and slipped in among the flock while they were out grazing. The shepherd didn't notice, and in the evening he penned the wolf in with the other sheep. So far all had gone to plan, but it happened that meat was needed for the table that night. Taking his knife, the shepherd went over to the pen and killed what he thought was one of his sheep. It turned out to be the wolf.

MORAL

It is dangerous to pretend to be something you are not.

THE TOWN MOUSE AND THE COUNTRY MOUSE

A COUNTRY mouse invited a friend from the town to visit him at his home in the fields. The town mouse was happy to accept, but was disappointed to find that all he was offered to eat was barley and roots. 'My poor friend,' he said, 'you live no better than an ant. You should see what I have at home. Come back to my place, and you'll eat like a king!' So they went off to the town together, and the country mouse was amazed by his friend's larder, which contained bread, oatmeal, cheese and fruit, and even honey and dates. As they sat down to enjoy these luxuries, he realized how deprived he had been. But just as they began to eat, someone came into the room and they quickly had to run and hide in a cramped little hole. When all was quiet, they returned to the food, but before they could eat anything someone else came in and again they had to run for cover. At this point the country mouse decided that he had had enough. 'Goodbye, my friend,' he said. 'I'm off. I'm sure you have a wonderful lifestyle, but you live in such danger! I'd rather eat simply and not have to look over my shoulder all the time.'

MORAL

Luxuries are not worth having at the expense of constant worry.

THE PROUD COCKEREL

TWO COCKERELS fought for the attention of the hens, and when one was defeated, he ran away to hide in a dark corner. His rival, full of his victory, climbed on to a high wall and crowed and crowed and crowed.

Just then an eagle swooped down, grabbed the noisy cockerel in his talons and carried it off. The other cockerel, safely out of view in his hiding-place, waited until the eagle had gone. Then he came out and got on with wooing the hens.

MORAL

Pride comes before a fall.

THE STAG AND THE LION

A THIRSTY stag went down to a pool and noticed his reflection in the water. He was very pleased to see how magnificent his antlers looked, but disappointed by his slender, weak-looking legs. Suddenly a lion came bounding towards him and he had to run for his life, with the lion breathing down his neck. The stag soon built up a lead, and kept it as long as the countryside was flat and open. While running through a wood, however, he got his antlers caught in some branches, which allowed the lion to catch up. 'What a fool I have been,' was the stag's last thought. 'My antlers, which I was so proud of, have caused my death – when my legs, which I despised, were saving my life.'

MORAL

We often think least of what we should value most.

THE CAUTIOUS FOX

A LION, who was too old and weak to hunt or fight for his food, decided that he must get it by another way. So he lay down in a cave, pretending to be ill, and whenever any animal came to visit him, he grabbed it and ate it.

A fox who had been watching the lion's trick came and stood outside the cave to inquire after the lion's health.

'Oh, I'm not at all well,' answered the lion. 'Why don't you come in and see me?'

'I'd like to,' said the fox, 'but I see many tracks going into the cave and not one coming out.'

MORAL

A wise man stops at a danger signal.

BIG AND LITTLE FISH

A FISHERMAN cast his net into the sea to see what he could catch. Many fish swam into his net, but when he pulled it in, the smaller fish slipped easily through the mesh and swam away to safety. Only the biggest fish remained for the fisherman to eat.

MORAL

The bigger and more important you are, the easier it is to trap you.

THE LION'S SHARE

A LION and a wild ass went hunting together, the lion using his strength and the ass his speed. When they had caught several animals, the lion divided the catch into three lots.

'I'll take the first lot,' he said, 'because, as king, I hold the highest position in the animal kingdom. And since I'm your equal partner in hunting, I'll take the second lot too. As for the third portion, I want that as well, so clear off before I get my teeth into you too.'

MORAL

Choose a partner carefully.

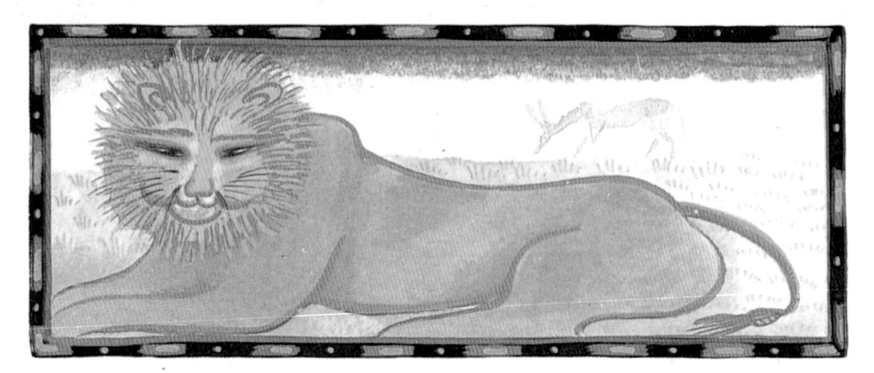

THE WOODMEN AND THE AXE

TWO WOODMEN were on a journey when one of them spotted an axe lying beside the road and decided to take it. 'Well,' said his friend, 'we have had a lucky find.' 'Don't say "we",' the other replied; 'say "You have had a lucky find".' They walked on, but then became aware that the owners of the axe were pursuing them. 'We are in trouble now,' said the man who had found the axe. 'Don't say "we",' replied the friend; 'say "I am in trouble" – for you had no intention of sharing it when you found it.'

MORAL

If we don't share our good fortune with our friends, we can't expect them to share our troubles.

OR:

Share and share alike.

THE LION AND THE ELEPHANT

ACCORDING to the ancient myths of Greece, the great god Prometheus created man and the animals, including the magnificent lion. But although the lion was big and strong, with razor-sharp teeth and claws, he complained that Prometheus had made him afraid of cockerels.

'Don't blame me,' said Prometheus. 'You have everything I could possibly give you. It's your own fault that you're afraid of cockerels.'

When the lion heard this he was terribly upset, and he worried and worried about being a coward. He became so miserable that he wanted to die. But then one day he met an elephant, and the two animals started to talk. While they were chatting, the lion noticed that the elephant kept flapping his enormous ears.

'What's the matter?' he asked. 'Can't you keep your ears still?'

Just then a gnat flew round the elephant's head.

'Do you see that tiny buzzing creature?' the elephant said, flapping his ears again furiously. 'If that wretched thing gets into my ear, I'm sure I'll go mad.'

The lion looked at the elephant's anxious expression and thought to himself, 'Well, things aren't as bad as I thought. I may be afraid of cockerels, but at least I'm not terrified of something as small as that gnat.'

MORAL

When you see another man's troubles, your own don't seem so bad.

HOW THE TORTOISE GOT ITS SHELL

ZEUS THREW a great feast for all the animals to celebrate his wedding, and everyone came except for the tortoise. When asked why he stayed away, the tortoise replied, 'I like my home more than anywhere else, so I don't leave it without a good reason.'

Zeus was so annoyed with the tortoise's excuse that he made him carry his home with him wherever he went.

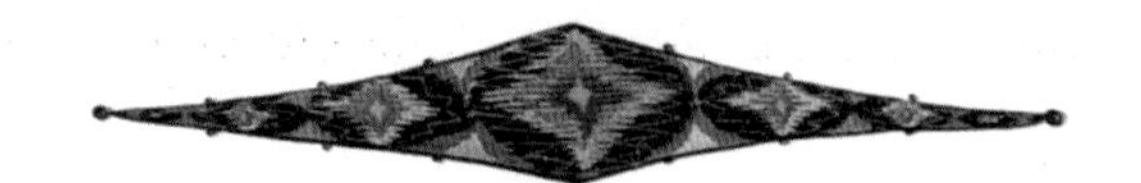

THE HIDDEN TREASURE

AN OLD FARMER, who wanted his sons to be successful farmers when he was gone, called them to him as he lay dying. He said to them, 'My boys, I'm about to leave this world. I've hidden something in the vineyard and I want you to search for it when I'm gone. If you do, you'll find everything I have to give you.'

The sons thought that their father meant there was some sort of treasure hidden in the vineyard and, after he died, they took out their spades and dug up every inch of soil. They couldn't find any treasure, but in the summer, because they had dug around the vines so thoroughly, they were rewarded with a bumper crop of grapes.

MORAL

The fruits of hard work are the best treasure of all.

A LESSON IN STRENGTH

A FARMER whose sons were always quarrelling tried to make them see how pointless their arguing was. But no matter what he said, they still bickered. So he decided to show them what he meant.

He took a bundle of sticks, handed it to them and told them to try to break it. They each tried but couldn't manage it. Then he untied the bundle and handed them the sticks one by one. This time they broke them easily.

'It's the same with you, my children,' he said. 'When you stay together you make a strong team. But if you break up and quarrel, you are easily beaten.'

MORAL

United we stand; divided we fall.

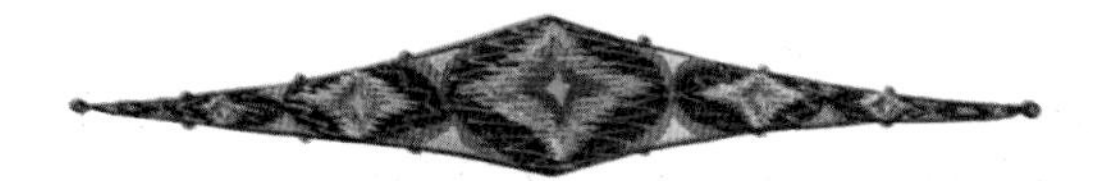

THE NOISY FROG

A LIONESS was lazing in the sun, when she was startled by a loud croak from a frog. 'What a large animal that must be,' she thought, and kept one eye open as she rested. The frog continued to croak noisily, and the lioness grew more nervous and restless. Eventually she could stand it no longer, and prowled about the pond, following the sound of the croaking. She soon found the frog behind a large leaf. 'All that worry,' she said, angrily, 'and it was only you,' and she crushed the noisy frog with her paw.

THE CAGED BIRD

THERE WAS ONCE a bird in a cage who would sing only at night. A bat who was passing by heard her and asked her why she never sang during the day.

'I used to sing in the daytime,' she explained sadly, 'but then I was captured. Now I've learned my lesson – it's too dangerous to sing during the day. So that's why I sing only at night.'

'It's a bit late for being careful now,' answered the bat. 'You should have thought about it before you were caught.'

THE MISER

A MISER sold everything he had, took the gold he received in exchange and melted it down into a single lump. He buried this in a secret place, but would go there every day to gloat over his hoard. These frequent visits were noticed by one of his men, who went there at night and stole the gold. The next day the miser paid his usual visit and found, to his horror, that the gold was gone. A neighbour, finding him groaning loudly and tearing out his hair, asked him what the matter was. Then, having heard the miser's tale of woe, the man said, 'Don't take it so hard. Why not just put a brick in the hole and make believe you still have your treasure? After all, you won't be any worse off than you were before, because even when you had the gold it wasn't any use to you.'

MORAL

A treasure which can't be enjoyed is not worth having.

THE HARES AND THE FROGS

THE HARES held a meeting at which they complained about the unhappiness of their lives. Danger surrounded them on every side, and there was nothing they could do against the humans, eagles, dogs and other hunting animals, all of which were killing hares every day. They argued that for them, the most timid of creatures, life was not worth living, and that it was preferable to put an end to it. Having all agreed, they ran together to a nearby pool with the intention of drowning themselves.

A group of frogs were sitting on the bank, and when they heard the hares coming they leapt into the water and hid. Seeing this, one of the older hares, who was wiser than the rest, called out, 'Stop, all of you, let's not do anything rash. These frogs are actually afraid of us hares, so they must be even more timid than we are.'

MORAL

Life does not seem so bad when there's someone worse off than you are.

THE FOOLISH MICE

A SNAKE and a weasel once shared a house, where they often went hunting together for mice. But one day they started to fight each other, and when the mice saw what was happening, they boldly walked out of their holes in search of food. As soon as the snake and the weasel spotted them, they stopped fighting and turned on the mice again.

MORAL

The hunted should always fear the hunter.

THE FROGS WITHOUT A KING

THE FROGS asked Zeus if he could appoint a king for them. They wanted a ruler, but couldn't choose one from among themselves. Amused by the simple frogs, Zeus dropped a block of wood into their pond, crying, 'Here is your king!' The frogs leapt out of the way, frightened by the splash it made. After a few minutes, when they saw that it did not move from the bottom of the pond, they cautiously crept back to investigate. They soon became tired of the block of wood and went back to Zeus.

'It's not a very dignified king,' they complained. 'Haven't you got anything better for us?'

By now Zeus was impatient with them. 'You don't deserve a better ruler!' he roared. Angrily, he sent a water snake to be their king but it was interested only in eating as many of the frogs as it could catch. And so those that remained were forced to run away to live in another pond.

MORAL

It is better to have a harmless ruler than a tyrant.

THE SPENDTHRIFT AND THE SWALLOW

A SPENDTHRIFT, who had wasted all his money and had nothing left but the clothes he was wearing, saw a swallow one day in early spring. Thinking that summer had come, and that he wouldn't be needing his coat any longer, he went out and sold that too. Soon afterwards, however, the weather turned bitterly cold again, and one day, while thinking wistfully of his coat, he came across the frozen body of the swallow. 'You wretched bird,' he said, 'thanks to you I too am freezing to death.'

MORAL

One swallow does not make a summer.

OR:

Never do anything drastic without first weighing all the evidence.

THE CAMEL

ON FIRST seeing a camel, people were terrified and ran away. As time went on, however, they realized that this was a gentle animal and could be approached safely. When they also discovered that nothing could anger it, they soon began to despise it, and eventually they harnessed it and even allowed their children to drive it about.

MORAL

Familiarity breeds contempt.

THE CLEVER DOG

A DOG was lying asleep in a farmyard when he was suddenly attacked by a wolf. The wolf was just about to devour him when the dog shouted, 'Don't eat me just yet. I'm thin and scraggy at the moment. But if you wait a little while, my master and his family are going off to a wedding. When they come back, they'll bring me all sorts of delicious titbits. Then I'll make a better meal for you.'

The wolf agreed to postpone his meal and went away. Some time later he returned to the farm. He found the dog asleep high up on a hayloft and called out to him to come down and keep his promise.

But the dog shouted down from the safety of his rooftop, 'You're too late. But if you ever find me sleeping on the ground again I shall deserve to be eaten!'

MORAL

A wise man learns from his mistakes.

THE PROUD FIR TREE

ONE DAY a fir tree and a thorn bush were arguing. The thorn bush was angry, as the fir was singing its own praises. 'I am tall and handsome and will be used for building such important things as church roofs and ships. How on earth can you compare yourself with me?'

'But think of the sharp axes and saws that will cut into you,' said the thorn bush, 'and then you'll wish you were like me.'

MORAL

Do not be proud of your beauty: it may be your downfall.

THE DOG, THE COCK AND THE FOX

A dog and a cock were travelling companions. When night fell, the cock flew up into a tree for safety, and the dog found a hollow below in which to sleep. At dawn the cock stood on a branch and gave a loud crow, which brought a vixen to the foot of the tree. She greeted the crow and invited him to come down, saying that she would very much like to meet the owner of such a splendid voice.

The cock, after a moment's thought, told the vixen that she should wake the porter, who was asleep below, and ask him to open the door. Then, said the cock, he would be right down. The vixen was just looking for this porter when out sprang the dog and chased her away.

MORAL

Discretion is the better part of valour.

THE JACKDAW WHO CHEATED

ZEUS DECIDED that the birds should have a leader, so he announced that the most handsome bird would reign over the others, and he set a day when they should all parade before him.

All the birds gathered on the beach to preen themselves for the ceremony. The plain jackdaw was determined to be king, so he borrowed feathers from the other birds and fastened them to his own. Dressed in his motley plumage he strutted about on the sand in front of Zeus and made a fine display. Seeing how impressed Zeus was, the other birds angrily plucked off his borrowed feathers until he was just a plain jackdaw again. Then Zeus chose another bird to be king.

MORAL

Dressing up in borrowed finery does not change who you really are.

THE FROG AND THE LAND RAT

A LAND RAT had the misfortune of becoming friendly with a frog, who played a nasty trick on him. Before they went off to look for food, the frog tied one of the rat's feet to one of his own. All was well at first, but when they came to a pond the frog dived in. He was in his element, but the poor rat, who was not, quickly became full of water and drowned. However, his body floated to the surface, and was seen by a kite that was flying overhead. Before the frog could untie the knot, the bird had seized the body of the rat in its talons and hoisted it into the air. So the frog, still fastened to the rat by his leg, was carried off and eaten as well.

MORAL

Those who do evil deeds come to bad ends.

THE AMBITIOUS JACKDAW

AN EAGLE swooped down from high in the air and carried off a lamb. A jackdaw, seeing this, was envious of the eagle's strength and tried to copy it. He flew high into the air and came shooting down on to the back of a sheep. His claws got caught in its woolly fleece and he beat his wings furiously in his efforts to release them. This attracted the attention of the shepherd, who ran over and caught him.

The shepherd clipped the jackdaw's wings, to prevent it from getting away, and that evening took it home with him. When his children asked what kind of bird it was, the shepherd smiled and said, 'I know he's a jackdaw, but *he* seems to think he's an eagle.'

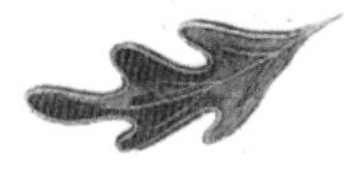

MORAL

Those who overreach themselves risk both misfortune and mockery.

THE FOX AND THE STORK

A STORK, who had just arrived from another country, was invited to dinner by a fox. The stork was delighted to be asked and went to the fox's home, feeling good and hungry. When she got there she discovered that the fox has prepared some clear soup and served it up in dishes that were so shallow she could not get her long beak in. She had to watch her host while he tucked in, and when he had finished, she went home, still hungry.

Next day the stork invited the fox to dine with her. The fox accepted the invitation, but when he arrived he found that she had prepared some thick soup which she served in tall jars. She stuck in her beak and really enjoyed her meal while the fox, almost fainting with hunger and unable to get his snout in, had to sit and watch.

When she had finished she smiled at him. 'I'm only following your example,' she said.

MORAL

Treat others the way you like to be treated yourself.

TWO OF A KIND

A MAN bought as ass at a market and took it home to run in the field with his other animals. Ignoring the rest, the new ass went to stand by the meanest and laziest of all the asses. The man took it back to the market and complained to the farmer who had sold it to him.

'But how can you tell?' asked the farmer. 'You've hardly given it a chance.'

'I don't need any more proof,' said the man. 'I can tell what it's like by the companion it chose.'

THE MONKEY AND THE FISHERMEN

FROM HIGH in a tree a monkey watched as some fishermen were casting their net into the river. He saw them catch several fish, and thought how easy it looked. So when they went off to eat their lunch, leaving their net unattended, he decided to imitate them. It wasn't as simple as it looked, however, and soon the monkey was up to his neck in water and getting entangled in the net. Close to drowning, he said to himself, 'This serves me right for trying to fish when I don't know how.'

MORAL

Each to his own.

THE SHEPHERD'S MISTAKE

A SHEPHERD was tending his flock near the shore, watching the ships sailing across the calm sea. He decided that he wanted to be a merchant sailor, so he bought a cargo of dates and set sail. That night a violent storm blew up, and the terrified shepherd threw all his dates overboard. The storm continued for many hours, but eventually the shepherd managed to steer the battered ship back to shore.

Many years later he was tending his sheep in that same place beside the sea. Another shepherd commented on how calm the sea looked. 'Ah, well,' replied the shepherd. 'I expect it is waiting for more dates.'

THE SELFISH HORSE

A MAN set off on a journey with many baskets, and he took both his horse and his donkey to carry the load. But the little donkey could not carry all her burden, and she begged the horse to take some of it for her. The horse was quite comfortable with his baskets, and refused. Soon the tired donkey could walk no further, and she lay down in the road and refused to move. The man put all the donkey's baskets on the horse's back and carried on his way. 'I wish I had helped the donkey a little,' wailed the horse. 'Now I have to carry the whole burden alone.'

MORAL

A burden shared is a burden no longer.

THE GRATEFUL EAGLE

A SMALL boy found a magnificent eagle caught in a trap. He thought that the bird was too beautiful to be killed, so he let it go.

A few days later the eagle saw the boy sitting at the bottom of an old wall. It flew down and snatched the boy's headband off his head. Angrily, the boy jumped up and chased the bird, who dropped the headband on the ground and flew away. The boy picked it up and made his way back to the wall.

When he got there he discovered that the wall had collapsed at the exact spot where he had been sitting. Then he realized that the eagle had repaid him for having rescued it earlier.

MORAL

One good deed often follows another.

THE CROW AND THE GODS

A CROW got caught in a snare and prayed to Apollo for help, vowing that he would offer incense to the god if he would help him to escape. When his prayer was answered, however, he failed to keep his promise.

Later the crow was caught again, and this time he appealed to Hermes, promising him a sacrifice. He was disappointed to hear Hermes reply: 'Miserable bird, how do you expect me to trust you after cheating Apollo?'

MORAL

Ingratitude shown to one benefactor makes it hard to find another.

SOMETHING OUT OF NOTHING

ONE DAY Heracles was walking along a path when he came across a small apple lying on the ground. Instead of stepping over it, he kicked it aside, but it didn't roll away; to his astonishment, it doubled in size. He kicked it again, and again it doubled in size. This made Heracles angry, so he gave it another, sharp kick. This time the apple grew so big that it blocked the path.

As he stood staring at it in confusion, Athena appeared before him. 'The apple is the spirit of strife and contention,' she explained. 'If you fight it, it will simply grow bigger.'

MORAL

Don't make a large problem out of a small one.

THE PARROT AND THE CAT

A man bought a parrot and took her home, where he allowed her to fly all round his house. The parrot settled in very quickly. The day after she arrived, the house cat came across her perched on the mantelpiece, chattering away quite happily to herself. The cat was most put out, and asked the parrot, in a rather frosty voice, who she was and where she had come from. The parrot replied that the master had just bought her.

'Well,' said the cat, 'you do have a nerve. Fancy a newcomer like you making such a racket, when I, who was born in this house, am not allowed even to miaow. If I do, my master gets furious and chases me away.'

'Well,' replied the parrot, 'my advice to you is to go and find yourself a new family. You see, the people of the house don't mind my voice, but I'm afraid it seems they don't like yours.'

MORAL

It is better to find people who like you
than to stay among those who don't.

THE DOG IN THE MANGER

THERE WAS once a dog who stood guard over a manger full of barley. It could not eat the barley itself, but it was determined to stop the zebra, who could eat it, from coming near.

MORAL

The greatest selfishness is to stop others from having what you don't want yourself.

THE LIONESS AND THE VIXEN

A VIXEN commented to a lioness one day, 'You're not as mighty as you think. You never manage to give birth to more than one cub at a time.'

'Maybe,' said the lioness quietly, 'but that one cub is always a lion.'

MORAL

It's quality, not quantity, that counts.

AN ASS IN A LION'S SKIN

AN ASS came across a lion's skin and dressed himself up in it. He then went around frightening the other animals, who all took him to be a lion. Delighted with the effect of his performance, he brayed loudly. This sounded familiar to the fox, who saw through his disguise. 'So it's you, is it?' he said. 'I would have been frightened myself if I hadn't heard your voice.'

MORAL

Those who pretend to be what they are not always give themselves away in the end.

THE PIG AND THE SHEEP

A PIG came to a place where sheep were grazing and decided to hang around with them. When the shepherd found him and tried to take him away, the pig squealed in alarm and struggled. The sheep were scornful. 'He often grabs hold of us and drags us off,' they said, 'and we don't make a lot of fuss.' 'I dare say you don't,' said the pig, still struggling, 'but that's different. With you all he's after is your wool, but with me it's my meat.'

MORAL

There is cause for alarm when it's your life, not just your property, at stake.

THE WISE MARTIN

WHEN MISTLETOE first began to grow on oak trees, its glue was used to make traps to catch birds. One wise martin realized the danger and warned the other birds that they should tear from the trees all the mistletoe they could find. The other birds laughed at the martin for making such a fuss, and took no notice of her advice. Despairing, she flew off to the trap-setters and asked if she could live with them. They praised her common-sense and welcomed her into their homes. Soon she was nesting safely in the eaves of their houses, while the other birds went on being caught by the traps of mistletoe glue.

MORAL

Be prudent and you will live a longer life.

MERCURY AND THE WOODMAN

A WOODMAN was working beside a river when his axe slipped out of his hands into the deep water. This was a disaster, and his cries of grief were heard by the god Mercury, who came to see what all the fuss was about. Hearing the man's story, the god felt sorry for him and dived into the water. He came back with a golden axe, and asked the man if this was the one he had lost. The man said no, and Mercury dived in again, reappearing with a silver axe. Was this it? 'No, that's not it either,' said the woodman. Finally the god came up with the missing axe, and the woodman was very thrilled and grateful. His honesty had so impressed Mercury that he let him keep the other too axes as well.

His friends were amazed when they heard about this, and one of them thought he would see if it would work for him too. He went to the river-bank, started felling a tree and let his axe slip out of his hands. He wailed loudly and, just as before, Mercury appeared, heard the man's story, dived in and came back up with a golden axe. 'That's it, that's it,' said the woodman, reaching for his prize. But he didn't get it, and lost his own axe too, because Mercury was so shocked by his behaviour that he refused to fetch it.

MORAL

Honesty is the best policy.

THE GOOSE THAT LAID THE GOLDEN EGGS

A MAN and his wife owned a goose which laid a golden egg every day. Instead of appreciating how lucky they were, they started looking for a way to get rich more quickly. Thinking that there must be a lot of gold inside the goose, they decided to kill the bird so as to get it all at once. Inside, however, the goose was just like any other, so they got no big treasure, and no more golden eggs.

MORAL

Don't let greed lead you to throw away what you already have.

OR:

Much wants more and loses all.

THE MEAN BEES

THE BEES wanted to keep their honey for themselves and did not want men to have any of it. So they went to Zeus and asked him to give them the power to sting to death anyone who dared to go near the honeycombs.

Zeus was so angry with them for their meanness and unkindness, he ordered that not only should they lose their stings whenever they used them on anyone, but they should also lose their lives.

MORAL

Selfishness brings its own punishment.

THE CRAB AND HER SON

A MOTHER CRAB, anxious to do the best for her son, told him to concentrate on walking straight instead of sideways. This was very difficult for the young crab, who also felt his mother was being rather unfair. 'Show me,' he said in frustration. 'Walk straight yourself, and I'll copy you.'

MORAL
Example is better than precept.
OR:
The best teaching is by example.

THE TRAVELLER AND FORTUNE

Exhausted after a long journey, a traveller lay down and went to sleep – right next to a deep well. Just as he was about to fall in, Dame Fortune touched him on the shoulder and said: 'Please wake up, sir, and move away from the well. If you fell in, it wouldn't be your carelessness that got the blame, but me, Fortune.'

THE HAWK, THE KITE AND THE PIGEONS

A COLONY of pigeons who lived in a dovecot were being terrorized by a kite, which would suddenly swoop down and carry one of them off. They had the idea of inviting a hawk to come and live with them and protect them from their enemy. They soon regretted their decision, however, because the hawk killed more of them in one day than the kite had in a year.

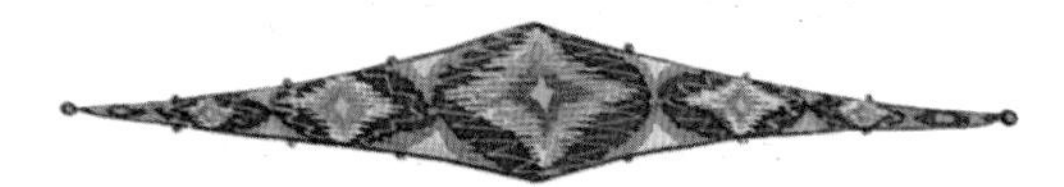

MORAL

Choose your allies carefully.

THE JEALOUS CAMEL

A MONKEY got up in front of a gathering of animals and started to dance. His audience clapped so loudly and paid him so many compliments that a camel standing in the crowd grew jealous. Thinking that he could get just as much attention, the camel walked out in front of the crowd and tried to dance like the monkey.

But the clumsy camel couldn't dance at all, and he looked so idiotic as he shuffled around that the angry crowd booed him and pushed him away.

MORAL

Don't try to be something that you're not.

1990

THE MAN AND HIS WIG

ONE DAY a gust of wind lifted a man's wig from his head and blew it away. The passers-by laughed at the man, but he replied with a smile: 'It's not surprising that I can't keep my hair on, because it doesn't grow there – and the man to whom it belonged couldn't keep it on his head either.'

MORAL

Never be ashamed of something that you do not bring upon yourself.

THE CAT'S TRUE NATURE

A CAT fell in love with a handsome man, and begged Aphrodite to change her into a human being. The goddess felt sorry for the cat and agreed, provided the cat would give up all her feline ways. Eagerly the cat promised she would, and so Aphrodite transformed her into an enchanting girl. The man was so struck by her beauty that he married her there and then.

As the newly wed couple sat together at their fireside, the goddess sent a mouse to run between the girl's feet. The excited girl pounced on the mouse – and then remembered her promise. But it was too late. Before she could apologise, Aphrodite had changed her back into a cat.

MORAL

Changing your looks will not turn you into a different person.

THE EXILED JACKDAW

A LARGE JACKDAW despised the other members of the flock because they were all smaller than him. He went off to find some crows and asked if he could live with them instead. At first the crows agreed, but when they discovered that the jackdaw looked and sounded different to them, they turned on him and pecked him.

The jackdaw realized he was not welcome, so he returned to his relations. But the other jackdaws, who were angry at the way he had insulted them, wouldn't allow him back, and so the foolish jackdaw had to live on his own.

MORAL

Don't expect those you have insulted to welcome you back.

THE WISE CICADA

A CICADA sat chirping in a tree while a hungry fox sat underneath, thinking up a plan to catch her and eat her. The fox looked up at the cicada and spoke to her, showering her with compliments about her musical voice. Then he suggested that the cicada should come down so that he could see how beautiful she was.

The cicada, however, was too clever to fall into the fox's trap. Instead she broke off a leaf and dropped it. Thinking it was the cicada herself, the fox dashed forward to catch it, and realized he had been tricked.

'I knew you were lying,' said the cicada. 'You see, I've been on my guard against foxes ever since the day I saw cicadas' wings in a fox's droppings.'

MORAL

Wise people learn from their neighbours' mistakes.

THE CRAB AND THE FOX

A CRAB left his home on the sea-shore and wandered inland. He came to a lush green field which he liked the look of and thought he would stay there for a while. But he was seen by a hungry fox, who had no difficulty catching him. Just as he was about to be devoured, the crab said, 'This is my own fault. I had no business leaving my seaside home and thinking I could live on the land.'

MORAL

Be content with your lot.

THE GREEDY ANT

THERE WAS once a farmer who was not happy with what he had himself and kept stealing his neighbours' crops. His greed made Zeus so angry that he changed him into the tiny insect that we now call the ant. But even though his body was changed, his character remained the same. He and all his kind still go to and fro, collecting other people's wheat and barley, and storing it up for themselves.

MORAL

Once a thief, always a thief.

THE FOX AND THE MASK

A CURIOUS fox crept into an actor's house and rummaged through all his things to see what he could find. In a trunk full of costumes he came across a wonderful mask shaped like a hobgoblin's head, which had been made by a talented artist. The fox held it up in his paws to admire it and said, 'What a magnificent head! It's a pity it has no brain it it.'

MORAL

A good brain does not always go with good looks.

THE BOY BATHING

A BOY got out of his depth while bathing in a river and was close to drowning. A passing traveller, who had heard his frantic cries for help, came to the riverbank and told the boy that it was very careless of him to have got into deep water. 'Please,' said the boy, 'help me first and tell me off afterwards.'

MORAL

In a time of crisis give assistance, not advice.

THE FROGS AND THE WELL

A PAIR of frogs lived in a marsh, but one summer it dried up and they went off to look for another place to live. They came to a deep well, and looked down into the water. 'That looks lovely and cool,' said one of the frogs. 'Let's jump in and make it our home.'

'Just a minute,' said the other. 'Supposing this well dries up too, how would we ever get out?'

MORAL

Think twice before you act.

THE SHIPWRECK

A RICH MAN took a valuable cargo on a voyage across dangerous seas. A storm soon blew up and the ship went down, throwing the passengers into the sea. They all began to swim for their lives, except the rich man, who raised his arms to heaven and promised his goddess Athena all kinds of riches if she would save him. The other passengers swam to pieces of wreckage and clung to them, and they shouted to the praying man, 'Don't leave it to the goddess to save you; swim for yourself.'

MORAL

The gods help those who help themselves.

THE TWO THIEVES

A WOLF stole a sheep from its flock, and was carrying it off to his lair when a lion sprang out at him from behind a bush. The wolf dropped the sheep and backed away, and the lion started to carry off the sheep. 'But you can't take it!' cried the wolf indignantly. 'That's *my* sheep.'

The lion only laughed. 'No it isn't,' he replied. 'It belongs to the shepherd, and you stole it. And now I'm stealing it from you.'

MORAL

One thief is as bad as another.

THE GREEDY DOG

A DOG was crossing a river with a piece of meat in his mouth. He saw his reflection in the water and thought it was another dog carrying what looked like a bigger piece of meat than his own. Straight away the dog dropped his meat and made a grab for the larger piece. Of course, he ended up with nothing, for his own piece was swept away by the river and the other was just a reflection.

MORAL

Greedy people end up with less.

A LESSON IN HUMILITY

A VAIN MAN read out to Aesop some long and dull essays he had written, and asked the wise man for his opinion. 'I'm very proud of my work,' said the man, 'but do you think I'm too boastful?'

'I think you are right to compliment yourself so much,' replied Aseop, 'for no one else will ever praise you.'

THE DISHONEST DOCTOR

AN ELDERLY woman, who lived in a house full of beautiful paintings and ornaments, asked her doctor to treat her sore eyes. The doctor came and put ointment on her eyelids, but while she sat with her eyes closed, he stole one or two of her valuable possessions. Each time he visited, he took another item, until the old woman's house was almost bare.

One day he arrived to treat her, but he found two policemen waiting to arrest him.

'I'm not a thief!' he protested.

'I didn't say you were a thief,' said the old lady, 'but you are a bad doctor. Before you cured my eyes, I could see all my belongings. Now I can't see any of them.'

MORAL

A thief will always be caught out.

THE FOX AND THE GRAPES

A HUNGRY fox saw some delicious-looking bunches of grapes hanging from a vine which had climbed along the branch of a tree. He jumped as high as he could, but was unable to reach them. In the end he gave up and walked off, saying, 'I thought they were ripe, but in fact I see they are sour.'

MORAL

Those who can't have something will often try to save face by saying it's not worth having.

THE WILD BOAR AND THE FOX

A FOX saw a wild boar sharpening his tusks on a tree-trunk, and was puzzled. 'Why are you doing that?' he asked. 'The hunters aren't out today, and you are not in any danger.' 'That's true', replied the boar, 'but when danger does come I will need them immediately, and there will be no time to sharpen them then.'

MORAL

Be prepared.

THE DETERMINED TORTOISE

A TORTOISE and a hare got into an argument about which of them could run the fastest. They decided that the best way to settle the matter was to have a race, so they fixed a time and a place to meet and then went their separate ways.

The hare was so confident that he was going to win that he didn't bother to start at the agreed time. Instead, he decided to take a nap. He told himself that when he woke, he could easily overtake the tortoise and win the race.

The tortoise set off on time and plodded along, without a single rest. On and on he went, past the sleeping hare, and eventually he crossed the finishing line. He had won the race.

MORAL

A slow and steady approach is often the best.

THE PACK-ASS AND THE WILD ASS

A WILD ASS was wandering about one day when he came across a pack-ass lying contentedly in the sun. Approaching him, the wild ass said, 'Well, you're a lucky fellow. I can see from your glossy coat that you are well provided for. I certainly envy you!'

Later that day he saw the pack-ass again, but this time with a heavy load on his back and being beaten with a stick by his driver. 'My poor friend,' said the wild ass, 'I'm not sure I do envy you after all, now that I see how much your comforts cost you.'

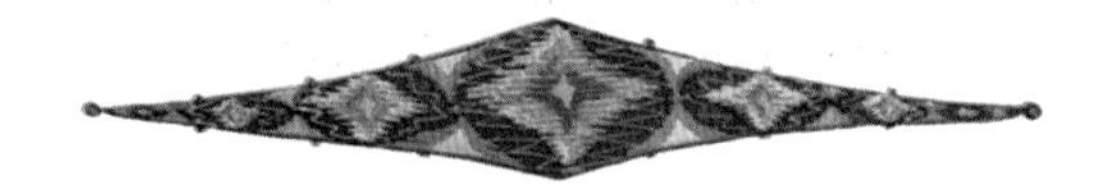

MORAL

Advantages bought at a high price are of doubtful value.

THE BEAR'S MESSAGE

TWO FRIENDS were travelling together when suddenly a bear came into view. One of them scrambled up a tree and hid in the branches. The other, realizing that the bear would be on top of him at any moment, threw himself down on the ground and pretended to be dead.

The bear came up to investigate, and sniffed the man all over. The man held his breath, for he had been told that a bear will not bother with a corpse.

Eventually the bear lost interest and ambled off, and the other man climbed down from his tree, rushed over to his friend and asked him what had the bear whispered in his ear.

'It told me,' the friend replied, 'that in future I shouldn't travel with friends who don't stand by me when there's danger.'

MORAL

True friends stay together, even through the bad times.

The Ant and the Dove

A THIRSTY ANT crawled down to the edge of a stream for a drink, but was carried away by the current. A dove who was flying by spotted the ant, broke off a twig and threw it into the water. The ant managed to crawl on to the twig and was washed safely on to dry land.

Later that day a hunter appeared with some sticks smeared with lime and started to set them in position to catch the dove. When the ant saw what he was doing she stung the man sharply on the foot. With a shriek of pain the hunter dropped the sticks and clutched his foot in agony. The dove, frightened by the noise, flew off.

MORAL

One good turn deserves another.

THE ASS AND THE WOLF

AN ASS who was grazing in a meadow caught sight of a wolf approaching and immediately pretended to be lame. The wolf asked him how he had come to be lame, and the ass replied that while going through a hedge he had trodden on a thorn. If the wolf was going to eat him, he said, it might be an idea for him to pull out the thorn with his teeth first. 'Otherwise it could stick in your throat and hurt you.' The wolf agreed and told the ass to lift up his hoof. As the wolf examined it, the ass gave him a violent kick in the mouth, knocking out his teeth, and ran away. 'It's my own fault,' said the wolf to himself. 'My father taught me how to kill, and I should have stuck to that instead of trying to be a doctor.'

MORAL

Every man to his own trade.

THE GUNDOG AND THE HARE

A DOG chased a hare out of a bush, and even though he was an experienced gundog, he found that the hare was streaking ahead, and no matter how hard he tried he could not catch up.

A goatherd, who had been watching the scene, laughed at the dog. 'How is it that a big, strong dog like you can't run as fast as an animal as small as that?' he cried.

'It's one thing,' answered the dog, 'running because you want to catch something, and quite a different thing running to save your life.'

THE REED AND THE OLIVE TREE

A REED and an olive tree were arguing about their strength and about how well each of them could survive the force of the wind and rain. The olive tree accused the reed of being weak and easily bent by even the tiniest puff of wind. The reed didn't say a word.

Soon afterwards a wind got up and started to blow strongly. The reed let itself be tossed around and bent by the gusts and survived the storm without any damage. The proud olive tree, on the other hand, tried to prove its strength by standing up to the wind and was broken in two as a result.

MORAL

It is better to be flexible than stubborn.

THE GRASSHOPPER AND THE ANTS

IN WINTER one fine day some ants were laying out their store of grain, which had become damp. A hungry grasshopper came along and begged them for something to eat. The ants were puzzled. 'What were you doing all summer?' they asked. 'Weren't you gathering a store of food for the winter, like us?' 'I never had time,' said the grasshopper, 'I was too busy singing.' 'Ah,' said the ants. 'Well, if you spent the summer singing, then why not spend the winter dancing?' – which they all thought extremely funny.

MORAL

Make hay while the sun shines.

OR:

If you don't look ahead, you will live to regret it.

JUMPING TO CONCLUSIONS

A LION and a man were walking along a path together when they came across a large stone at the side of the road. On the stone was carved a picture of a hunter pinning a frightened lion to the ground. The man pointed to the carving and joked, 'There's proof that we men are stronger than you.'

But the lion smiled. 'Not at all,' he replied. 'If lions could carve, you would find just as many pictures of men being eaten.'

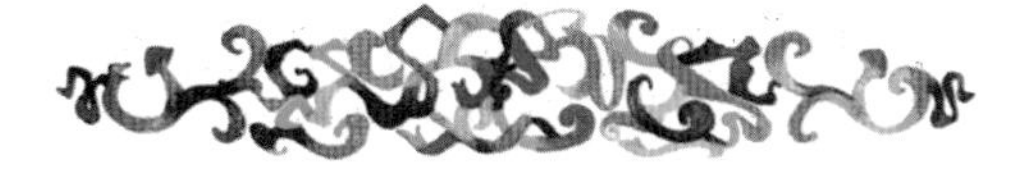

THE BALD MAN

A MAN, whose hair was going grey, had two mistresses, one young and the other old. The old one was ashamed of having a younger man for a lover, and when he was with her she pulled out as many of his black hairs as she could. The young woman, on the other hand, was embarrassed about having an old man as her lover, and she pulled out his grey hairs. In the end, the poor man was completely bald.

MORAL

You can't please everyone all the time.

When a Man Means Business

A pair of larks made their nest in a field of unripe corn and fed their chicks on the green shoots until the birds had grown their feathers and were ready to fly. Around this time the farmer inspected his field and saw that the corn was ripe.

'Perhaps I should ask all my friends to help me with the harvest,' he said.

One of the chicks overheard him and told its father. 'It's time for us to find another home,' said the chick.

'We don't need to move for a while,' replied the father. 'The person who relies on his friends to do a job for him is not too bothered about getting it done.'

A few days later the farmer visited the field again and saw the ears of corn dropping off in the heat of the sun.

'Tomorrow I must hire some men to harvest this corn and tie it up in sheaves,' he said.

'*Now* we had better move on,' said the lark to his young. 'A man really means business when he relies on himself rather than on his friends.'

1920

TRUE FRIENDS

A GREAT MAN once had a small house built for himself to live in. A passer-by remarked that it was rather small for such an important man. 'Why do you not build a grander house for your visitors?' she asked.

'Because my true friends will find it grand enough,' replied the man.

MORAL

True friends like you for what you are, not for what you own.

THE BELLY AND THE FEET

THE BELLY and the feet were arguing about who was the stronger. The feet insisted that they were far stronger than the belly because they carried it about all the time.

'That's true,' replied the belly, 'but if I stopped providing you with nourishment, you wouldn't be able to carry me at all.'

MORAL

People depend on one another more than they realize.

THE SUN AND THE WIND

THE NORTH wind and the sun got into an argument one day about who was the stronger. They agreed that the best way to decide the question was to see which of them could force a man to strip off his clothes.

First, the wind had a go. Its fierce gusts only made the man pull his clothes more tightly around him. Then it blew even harder and the man was so cold that he put on an extra layer. Eventually the wind gave up and let the sun try.

The sun started by shining with a gentle warmth, which made the man take off his overcoat. Then it sent out hotter rays, and the man soon took off his jacket. Finally it blazed with all its strength and the man, who could stand the heat no longer, stripped and went to swim in a nearby river.

MORAL

Persuasion is often more effective than force.

THE FOOLISH CROW

A CROW perched on the branch of a tree, holding in his beak a piece of meat. Before he could eat it a fox saw him and decided that he wanted the meat for himself. He stood under the tree and began to tell the crow what a handsome bird he was.

'With your looks,' said the wily fox, 'you should be king of the birds and you certainly could be if your voice was as impressive.'

The crow was so keen to prove that he had a good voice that he opened his beak and croaked for all he was worth. The piece of meat fell to the ground, where the fox quickly gobbled it up and said, 'And if you added brains to all your other qualities, you'd make a first-class king.'

MORAL

Vanity is the mark of a fool.

THE ASS AND HIS BURDENS

ONE DAY a pack-ass, carrying a heavy load of salt, stumbled and fell while crossing a stream. The salt was soaked, and by the time the ass had got back on to his feet, much of it had dissolved. The load, the ass noticed, was now considerably lighter, so when his master had driven him back for a fresh load, and they came back to the stream, the ass made a point of rolling in the water again. As before, the burden was lighter when he got up, and the ass felt very pleased with his discovery.

His master, seeing that this was going to be an expensive habit, decided to teach the ass a lesson. On their next trip he made a point of loading the ass with a huge quantity of sponges. His enormous burden was actually quite light, but when they came to the stream the ass repeated the trick. This time, however, he had difficulty getting up at all, for the sponges had soaked up gallons of water and his load was far heavier than before.

MORAL

You can play a good card once too often.

THE FROG'S WORDS OF WISDOM

ONE SUMMER'S day all the animals threw a party because they heard that the sun was going to be married. A frog hopped up and interrupted the dancing.

'You fools,' he said, 'what are you celebrating for? The heat from one sun alone is enough to dry up every pool. What do you think will happen if he marries and has a child who is just as powerful as he is?'

MORAL

When you celebrate, make sure it's worthwhile.

THE FLUTE-PLAYING WOLF

A YOUNG goat, who was walking along behind the rest of his friends, suddenly found himself face to face with a wolf. Before the wolf could pounce, the goat cried, 'I know you're going to make a meal out of me. But please grant my last wish and play the flute for me so that I can dance.'

The wolf agreed, and while he was playing and the goat was dancing, some dogs arrived, having heard all the commotion. They chased away the wolf, and the goat was able to run off after his friends.

'Serves me right,' said the wolf. 'I shouldn't have tried to be a flute-player when I had hunter's work to do.'

MORAL

Don't be distracted from what you set out to do.

THE AMARANTH AND THE ROSE

AN AMARANTH remarked to the beautiful rose that grew beside it, 'No wonder everyone is so enchanted by you. You are perfectly shaped, your petals are a glorious colour, and you have an exquisite perfume.'

'Thank you for the compliments,' replied the modest rose, 'but I live only for a short while, and even if no one cuts me, my beauty fades very quickly. You, on the other hand, bloom time after time, and always stay as fresh as you are now.'

MORAL

Don't envy perfect beauty: its life is all too short.

THE STAMMERING HUNTER

A HUNTER, who was trying to track down a lion, met a forester, who asked him what he was looking for. The hunter answered that he wanted to trap a lion, and asked the forester if he knew where the lion's lair was. The forester said that better still, he could show him the lion itself. At this the hunter turned very pale, and his teeth began to chatter.

'It's a-a-a-ll right,' he stammered, 'I'm only l-l-l-looking for its trail.'

MORAL

Deeds speak louder than words.

THE GNAT'S STICKY END

A GNAT settled on a lion's ear and said to the lion, 'I'm not afraid of you. I can do everything just as well as you can. I know, you'll say that you can scratch with your claws and bite with your teeth, but anyone can do that, so that's not every impressive. I'm really much stronger than you, and to prove it, I'll fight you.'

The gnat then latched on to the lion's face, viciously biting him around his nose. The lion tore at his face to try to knock off the gnat, but his paws were too big and clumsy, and eventually he admitted defeat.

The triumphant gnat gave a victorious cry and flew away delighted. But he was instantly caught in a spider's web, and as the owner of the web crept up to claim its meal, the gnat cried, 'Oh, isn't life unfair. Here I am, fresh from defeating the strongest creature in the animal kingdom, and now I'm about to be destroyed by nothing bigger than a spider.'

MORAL

Victory is often short-lived.

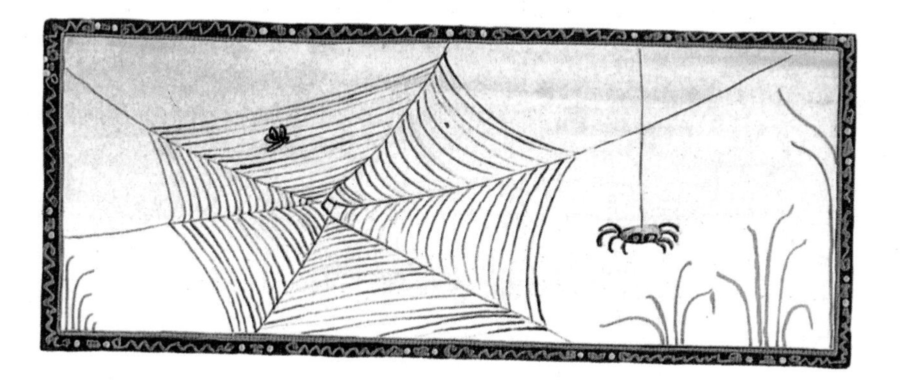

About the Author

We do not know whether Aesop actually existed or not, and whether he wrote the famous fables himself. Herodotus tells us that he worked as a slave in the house of Iadmon in the sixth century B.C., and other stories tell that he was ugly and lame. References to his existence can also be found in the Athenian writers such as Aristophanes, Xenophon, Plato, and Aristotle.

In many of the tales that have been handed down to us, the animals have human characteristics and convey simple moral lessons. Such stories are known as fables. The animals poke fun at human failings, revealing universal truths about human nature.

The earliest written versions of Aesop's fables date from the third century AD, and thereafter were translated into many different languages, with the earliest editions being produced for adults rather than children.

Despite the passing of many hundreds of years, these resoundingly simple and significant fables have survived, and are as relevant and entertaining today as they must have been at their first telling.

Other Titles in the Series

PETER PAN AND WENDY

J. M. Barrie
Illustrated by Michael Foreman

Ever since Peter Pan first flew in through Wendy Darling's nursery window and took the three children to Neverland, J.M. Barrie's enchanting story of the boy who never grew up has delighted generations of young readers. Michael Foreman's imaginative illustrations depicting the lost boys, the magical island, the mermaids, fairies and pirates, bring new life to this classic tale.

THE WIND IN THE WILLOWS

Kenneth Grahame
Illustrated by Graham Percy

Kenneth Grahame's delightful story of Mole, Ratty, Toad and Badger is one of the greatest masterpieces of children's literature. Scenes of cheerful riverside picnics, mysterious snow-covered woods and the grand interiors of Toad Hall are beautifully captured by popular children's illustrator, Graham Percy, in this colour illustrated edition. An all-time favourite, loved by both adults and children.

TREASURE ISLAND

Robert Louis Stevenson
Illustrated by Justin Todd

Robert Louis Stevenson's classic tale combines danger and excitement in a fast-moving plot filled with mysterious maps, shipwrecks, smugglers, mutiny, menacing pirates and a hunt for buried treasure. This richly illustrated edition brings to life unforgettable heroes and villains, among them Long John Silver, Ben Gunn, Black Dog and the young narrator, Jim Hawkins.

THE LITTLE PRINCE

Antoine de Saint-Exupéry
Illustrated by Michael Foreman

Since its first publication fifty years ago, Antoine de Saint-Exupéry's whimsical tale has become a modern classic, attracting a devoted following in each successive generation. This newly-translated edition is accompanied by Michael Foreman's sensitive illustrations, evoking the haunting encounter between a pilot stranded in the Sahara desert and a strange, enchanting child.

THE RAILWAY CHILDREN

E. Nesbit
Illustrated by Dinah Dryhurst

The adventures of the Railway Children have thrilled and amused readers of many generations, and will continue to do so in this beautifully illustrated edition. Dinah Dryhurst has painstakingly researched the period setting, and the freshness of her watercolours and detail of her lively pencil sketches bring to life these remarkable children and their long golden summer of adventure.

BLACK BEAUTY

Anna Sewell
Illustrated by Dinah Dryhurst

Anna Sewell's moving story is one of the best-loved animal adventures ever written. She began to write *Black Beauty*, her only book, in 1871, having been given only eighteen months to live. She spent the next six years confined to her house, writing the book that she hoped would induce kindness, sympathy and an understanding treatment of horses .

LITTLE WOMEN

Louisa May Alcott
Illustrated by Dinah Dryhurst

In 1868 Louisa May Alcott began to write a novel based on her own childhood. *Little Women* is a touching and sensitive portrayal of the lives of four young sisters growing up during the time of the American Civil War. Louisa May Alcott's vivid descriptions of their many trials and triumphs are moving, humorous, and unforgettable.

THREE MEN IN A BOAT

Jerome K. Jerome
Illustrated by Paul Cox

One hundred years after it first appeared, Jerome K. Jerome's classic account of an eccentric journey up the Thames by rowing boat remains as popular as ever. Paul Cox, the illustrator, retraces the erratic progress of J., Harris, George and Montmorency the dog and records the highlights and low points of their accident-prone voyage.